BOONE

A NOVEL

Brooks Hansen
&
Nick Davis

SUMMIT BOOKS
New York   London   Toronto   Sydney
Tokyo   Singapore

SUMMIT BOOKS
SIMON & SCHUSTER BUILDING
ROCKEFELLER CENTER
1230 AVENUE OF THE AMERICAS
NEW YORK, NEW YORK 10020

Designed by Carla Weise/Levavi & Levavi
Manufactured in the United States of America

1   3   5   7   9   10   8   6   4   2

Library of Congress Cataloging in Publication Data
Hansen, Brooks,
Boone : a novel / Brooks Hansen & Nick Davis.
p. cm.
I. Davis, Nick.   II. Title
PS3558.A5126B66   1990
813'.54—dc20   90-9624
CIP

ISBN 0-671-68108-7

TO OUR PARENTS

Contents

GOSPEL SINGERS SHOULD SING GOSPEL.
—a show-biz maxim

PROLOGUE

The Stage

New York, 1967

Hugh Gardiner

We do with history as we please. That's what's so distressing. I
had a letter from a student of mine some years ago, from England
where she was living. She said that she'd seen a painting of
Boone's in one of the prop rooms at the BBC and that it made her
think of me. She was recalling the evenings we all used to spend
driving into the city to see Boone's performances and then returning the same night for tea at my home. That was in late 1967,
and she wanted to know what had happened to Boone since then.
She was aware of his movie and the play, and the book, of course,
but she said she'd heard he'd gone mad, and she wanted to know
when.

Her question caught me quite off guard, I can say, but there was something I recognized in the way she asked it, or perhaps it was the idea itself, of Boone having lost his mind—it's strange, but there's a need for reassurance there, I think. It reminded me of the things my students would say whenever we'd come back from seeing him. They'd sit in my living room afterwards with their tea and call him things like relentless and cruel. They'd shake their heads and wonder what the purpose was of being so ruthless. And I always tried to tell them, don't think of him as fierce. When you see Boone perform, think of it as something like finding a diary. I said, Imagine yourself in a stranger's bedroom, looking at the books on their shelves, at the keepsakes and pictures on their bureaus and end tables. Imagine even sitting on their bed, lying there and resting your head on the pillow. But then finding underneath the pillow a diary. Would you open it? Perhaps no—perhaps—but the temptation is there, and I asked the students to imagine the temptation always there, of reading and understanding the most private and intimate feelings of every person they saw, because for Boone it was. In his letters to me, he would describe certain people's faces as "perfectly legible," or their movements and manners as "graphic." The question for him was always whether or not to look, and I think he did at first—and I said this to the students—Boone reads our faces and gestures avidly, not because he's ruthless, but because he simply can't imagine that such expressive things could really want to keep their secrets. And my students would say, yes, but if that's so, if his intentions are so innocent, then tell us why everything he finds is so ugly? Why doesn't he ever look at people's faces and find something beautiful there, because surely there must be something to comfort us?

I never answered them. I didn't think it was my place, but I've discovered there's a funny thing that happens to that question over time. If it just lingers there, and we never quite get the answers or comfort that we're asking for, then I suppose we end up having to comfort ourselves. Years pass, and it's no longer a question, why doesn't Boone ever reassure us? The question becomes, "When did Boone go mad?" I was very reluctant to write my old student back and tell her—he didn't ever, that's just it.

thin, slightly pinched, and all of a sudden you can see it, Boone gets Burton's mouth just perfect. So he finishes with the face, and then he does the body, the way he holds his shoulders, the way he moves his hands, his walk, everything he can think of until finally when he's finished, pacing around this dressing room with his glass of Irish whiskey in his hand, he is Richard Burton. It was an absolute metamorphosis. The audience, some of them start pounding on their tables they're so into it.

But he turns back to this kid Julian again, once he's set, and he asks if he'd like his autograph. He takes the kid's autograph book and starts flipping through it. He's being kind of glib, making little comments about all the names he recognizes, but then all of a sudden he stops cold, and at first you don't know what it is. He starts nodding his head. He sits back down in the chair and he pours himself some more whiskey, but his eyes never leave the book. He swallows the shot, then he looks up at Julian and the word comes out of his mouth like a vapor—"Olivier."

Eton Arthur Boone, transcribed, December 8, 1967—
RICHARD BURTON

[Looks at book again.] Strange. *[Considers.]* I wonder what Larry was wearing when he signed this. Do you remember? Was there a crown on his head when he wrote this, Julian, or was there a great big putty nose on his face? Who was he pretending to be? Because I'll let you in on a secret, my young friend, and it doesn't leave this room, but it's true—and pour me another drink, would you? *[Waits.]* I'll pour it myself then. *[Pours himself a drink. Returns to the mirror.]* Laurence Olivier is the shallowest man you will ever meet. Sometimes I think there is no Laurence Olivier. There are only clothes. There are costumes, crowns, elaborate makeup and then that purposeless face of his to put it on, but it's just a prop like everything else. He's all tricks, Julian, disguises and acrobatics, but he gives you nothing of himself ever, don't you see, because there's nothing there to give. How else do you think he's been able to do it, go from part to part like that without leaving a trace? It's that he's no character of his own for us to remember. He's like a tire pump—inexhaustible, but completely hollow. *[Swallows his drink in one gulp.]* Now pour me another, would you? *[Snaps twice.]*

Kelso Chaplin

We had no idea how ambitious and persistent he was going to be. You know comedians, they never want to stick with any idea too long, because they're afraid of losing you. But Boone, you could tell just by looking at him, he was there to explore. He was moving around the stage, and it was still clearly Burton, but something kind of animal was taking over. He was stalking. It was like watching a jackal go after his prey, except that Boone was hunting this man down from the inside. It was incredible. And you could feel it in the club too. This air had set in. Everybody was getting a little uncomfortable, they're not sure they really want to look at this thing, except they can't take their eyes off him. They had to know, Where's he headed? Where's he going? Because always, in every performance, there was this intense momentum, in every performance, a kind of steady crescendo that just kept building and building, until you knew that something had to give. Something was going to jam or bust or blow, and if you didn't look out, it could be dangerous. You could have Richard Burton's shot glass flying over your head.

Eton Arthur Boone, transcribed—RICHARD BURTON

[Standing, glaring out towards the audience, his focus fixed on a figure in the imaginary mirror before him.]

. . . I'll be there in everything I do, Julian, won't I, shining through every role I play, every jacket I wear, or crown—no King Arthur, no Alexander, only that—*[points into mirror]* Richard Burton. But don't blame me for it, Julian. Pity me, I did that for you. It's both our doing that I should shine so bloody bright. You've never been so tempting to seduce. The rewards have never been so grand, to be known from Rome to Hollywood, in London and Singapore, to have money and yachts, and the world's most beautiful woman at my beck and call for all the world to see, the whole world watching. Who could resist? Who but a cipher like Olivier? He knows nothing of desire, he hasn't the balls between his legs to feel it, but I have let it guide me, for longer than I can remember, in every gesture I have made, and I have been exposed for it. Look. *[Gestures easily towards mirror, indicating his reflection to Julian.]* I am unmistakable. Look how irrepressible is Richard Burton. Look in his eyes, Julian, and it's the same thing always—resignation. Look at his mouth—disgust and arrogance. Smell his breath—misery. And ask yourself why. "Why such contempt, Richard Burton? You've gotten what you wanted. Why such disdain?" *[Leans over, fingers on cheeks, stares at self in imaginary mirror.]* Because I'd no idea you were so easy. I'd no idea you'd cling like this. You should leave me now, Julian. Do. Get out of my dressing room if you know what's good for you. Leave me alone and tell the rest of them too. Out now, boy! *[Picks up glass.]* Leave me, dammit! Go! *[Hurls glass at the imaginary mirror, glass shatters on the back wall of the club. Blackout.]*

Linda Chaplin

Basically on any given night, you had two types of people in the club. The ones who left afterwards, never to return, and the ones who were going to keep coming back no matter what. And given the nature of what Boone was doing, that's certainly understandable. It's understandable that some people aren't always going to go for this sort of thing—maybe the imitation didn't click with them that night, or maybe they found the whole thing just too presumptuous and offensive. I mean, there's no doubt that Boone could be offensive. I remember taking some friends of mine one night, they were in from Madison, and Boone had done Diana Ross making love to the palms of her hands, and it was very awkward afterwards having to explain to them, you know, "He's not always like this."

But I actually think that in order to understand what Boone was doing, you really did have to see him more than once, because so much of it had to do with his sheer variety. I mean,

here was a performer who one night you could see doing the
Richard Burton, right, this very stagy sort of tongue-lashing,
but if you went back two days later, which Kelso and I actually
did, you'd see him doing just this beautiful piece on Sonny Liston, the professional boxer, which was absolutely heartbreak-
ing. And if you went again the next night, who knows what
you might get? Grace Kelly on the toilet? Kerouac mourning the
death of Neal Cassady? Maybe J. Edgar Hoover getting ready to
sodomize his page boy. It could be anything. The man was all
over the board.

But what I think was so interesting, right, was that even as
diverse as these routines may have seemed from certain perspec-
tives, there was also something about them that was very much
the same, and the more you went, the more you could see it—
Eton Boone had his own antenna. He had his own hook, right,
and if you were watching him with that in mind, you could
see—Liston, Burton, Hoover, whoever it was—Boone was doing
the same thing to each of them, and the best phrase I ever heard
for it came from a teaching assistant I had at Emerson, Clayton
Stern. It was very simple. Clayton used to say that Eton Boone
really knew how to put someone in his place. I love that, because
it's not just that Boone could knock someone down a few pegs—
which he could, obviously—it's that he was able to take these
well-known, public personalities and place them in very specific
settings and circumstances that just completely illuminated them,
where everything around them either seemed to reflect their
identity or provoke it, or threaten it, so that in essence what you
were watching was someone being made to confront himself. You
were watching someone having to choose himself all over again,
and what was always so disturbing, I think, was seeing how often
these people didn't want to do it. I mean, it makes sense, I guess—
people do hate being put in their place—but that's what Boone
was doing, right. That's sort of the service he was offering, and
I actually think that what started to be so thrilling about watching Boone wasn't really the celebrities so much or the imitations.
It was the idea that Eton Boone could do this to anyone he
wanted. You know, so look out, keep the house lights dim, right,
because it really got to the point where you felt like nothing was
stopping Boone, except for Boone, from coming out and doing
you.

Kelso Chaplin

The whiskey glass broke about a foot and a half above Sy's head, so there's chaos on the film. The lights black out, you can hear Sy going, "Oh, man," like he's been shot, and the audience, after a second or two of complete silence, literally explodes. But it's not a happy sound. Most of them are applauding, but a lot of them, even the ones who are clapping, are yelling, just hollering, so you hear this mass wail on the film. Sy finally regains his composure and gets the picture in focus. The camera goes back to the stage, but the whole thing's dark. You can just barely see this dark figure, this outline of Boone feeling his way off stage, bumping into things. Some of the people in front of us have stood up, so you can't see him coming up the aisle, and by the time the lights come up, he's gone. The crowd's still going wild, but it's just the bricks now.

I

San Diego

1 9 4 7 — 1 9 6 6

From RUTH, by Eton Arthur Boone*

When I was twelve, my mother and I ran away from home. We never shared our reasons why, but I think that most of them had to do with my father. I once pictured our house surrounded and cluttered by loose rope, wound slack around all the furniture and sitting in heaps on the rugs and stairs. Mom and I would try and clean it up. We'd tie as many ends as we could find to the back fender of the car and drive off. We wouldn't see, but the lines would fly and untangle behind us. The braids would untwine. The

---

*Ruth was first published in 1975 by Hardcastle, Inc., New York. Portions of *Ruth* are reprinted here by permission of the Estate of Eton Arthur Boone.

coils would whistle away like tiny cyclones, and all the knots would slip. And when the ropes were finally pulled tight and separate, Mom and I would follow them back on foot to see where they'd come from. They'd lead us to Dad, they'd all converge in one enormous snarl wrapped impossibly around his crotch.

I don't imagine anymore that all the ropes would lead to him. I'm sure that some were fastened elsewhere, some that Mom would follow, but there's very little I could ever know about where or what to. She was dying. Cancer had been creeping through her body for years, and I think that when she escaped with me that June, she may just have wanted one more chance to get away, far away, and make peace with life before it began to fade.

We would visit the Southwest, down into Sonora then up through Arizona, and we'd follow the Zuni River into New Mexico. She wanted to take her time, take close looks, and she wanted her paint boxes and canvases with her. She was going to do what she liked best, and it seems I should have felt blessed to be asked along, but I was too frightened. I thought she'd want to know things about Dad, things I knew very well but would never tell, for reasons I hadn't yet admitted, except for one—a sense I suffered quietly that when she understood what had happened, she would die. Our trip was a kind of tempting fate, and even before we left I could feel it spread out before me savagely, as the last moments I could spend alone with my favorite person on earth, and as an awful and gradual means for her to discover what I had done.

Claire Sullivan

Eton had the very same color eyes when he was a little boy as his mother, the very lightest blue, almost bleached, but they turned more gray and green when he got older. Blue's stayed the same as when she was a little girl, which was very lucky, I suppose. She wouldn't have made a very good Hazel. Her given name was Ruth, but Blue was Blue, from the very moment she was born.

I remember being upstairs once at the Lemon House in San

Diego and Eton was so young—well, he must have been five, because I think Blue was six or seven months pregnant with Toddy. She was wrestling with Eton, trying to get a sweater over his head, and he was singing a song while she was doing it. He was teasing her with a song about eating booger peas, and when he was singing it, I was almost certain I'd heard it before but I couldn't remember where exactly. But then it came to me. It was a song that the CCC boys used to sing when they were working on the projects near Sullivan South, but of course it wasn't about booger peas. It was about goober peas, and I think originally the Yankee troops used to sing it during their marches in the Civil War. But I told Eton that I'd first heard his little song when I used to visit his mother down at Sullivan South, and she was just a little girl, not much older than he was.

Sullivan South was the loveliest fieldstone house on a small branch of the Delaware with just acres and acres of smooth green land surrounding it, and up the road a bit when we were all very young there was a bridge being built by the CCC boys, and I told Eton how horrified his grandfather had been at the thought of these hooligans so near the property. He used to curse President Roosevelt and warn us never to go near these dangerous fellows, which was very silly. I remember Eleanor, Blue's older sister, she was a teenager at the time and very rambunctious. She used to trot by on her horse, and the men would take off their caps and bow as she passed.

But when Blue was very young, she would go down to the river banks and paint. She would sit all day with a pad on her knees and her little brushes—my mother used to say Blue was like a Beatrix Potter let outdoors. And when these boys came singing their songs and building their bridges, she painted them as well. You know, Eleanor and I saw these young boys as people to flirt with, and Uncle Edwin saw them as people to fend off for the sake of his little women. But Blue only saw more things to paint—that's all—like trees and the sky, and now these great big men in shirtsleeves and coveralls, singing about goober peas.

There was a painting of hers we still have somewhere, that I was always trying to find for Eton, of the river with just half a bridge going across, and the men on it, working. When I was little I'd always thought it was so funny that Blue hadn't minded the bridge just going halfway like that. It would've bothered me.

Uncle Edwin just loved the painting, though—pretended not to know what it was of. He put it in his bathroom, so he could look at it while he shaved. He put the most extraordinary frame on it too, carved wood and gilded, that he'd bought in Baltimore.

Joe Boone

Blue and I met in Philadelphia. It was late summer of 1945—I'd missed going to the Pacific by two weeks. A friend of mine from the Navy named Buzzy Kaulgren and I had three days' leave from our base in South Carolina, and we had to drive up to Philadelphia to drop off some old DeSoto for Buzzy's aunt. I drove the DeSoto.

It was at a dance, Saturday night. Buzz and I were in our uniforms. His family got us the invites—he was from back East—very posh affair with a big band and all the women in those dresses that keep going straight ahead even when the woman turns in another direction, these chicken coops the women had to wear back then. I remember Buzz and I walking around feeling like security guards. We felt like we should have been checking people's passes or something, but we were just two soldiers trying to kill an evening in Philadelphia.

But Buzz, he was a terrific dancer, hell of a dancer, so he was busy for most of the evening. He ditched me midway through for a girl he ended up getting engaged to named Mamie Bosomworth. Anyway, I didn't know how to dance—somehow my father had never gotten around to teaching me the fox-trot. We were too busy shooting snake tails, which doesn't mean you shoot the tail. It means you beat a snake against a rock, stretch it out flat and then stick the gun down its throat, see how close you can come to shooting the bullet right out the tip of the tail. That's what my father and I used to do, and that wasn't going to help me on the Main Line. So I had to assert myself socially. That's it. That's why we met. Not a single shot was fired.

Sounds corny, but it was at the punch bowl. She'd been there with some fella named Ned Barnes. Poor bastard, killed in Korea, but that night he'd gone on to some other party. So there we were, talking by the punch bowl, stiff as boards and I never felt so comfortable in my goddamn life. I told her right off about my family, Texas, my dad. This was the first time we met, you have to remember, and I'm telling her about my dad and how he made my mother sit in the back of the truck when we moved out to Los Angeles.

Blue didn't say anything. I did all the talking, but not just to fill the air. She was so lovely. She didn't carry herself the way the other women did. She could have been in a cotton dress out at Mount Tamalpais, out in one of the meadows where we ate an entire watermelon once—that was maybe a year after we first got out to California. But if she'd been in a cotton dress you couldn't have seen Blue's shoulders, which I almost told her right then and there were perfect. It was that kind of thing, that just meeting her right there I could have told her what perfect shoulders she had, or how I couldn't believe her eyes, how beautiful they were, and it wouldn't have been some kind of line. You don't meet people like that very often, and when you do, you fall in love. I fall in love.

I asked her to marry me thirteen days after we met. She wasn't quick to answer, but she wasn't slow either. I asked her, we'd gone to Chadds Ford together, by the Brandywine, and I asked her there to marry me.

Claire Sullivan

The Sullivans always had trouble understanding. They never quite got Joe. He has such a hard humor about him. I remember a number of us all having dinner together in New York just after they'd been engaged. None of the parents, but Blue and Joe, and Eleanor and her husband Tom, Alice, who was the oldest sister, and myself. Just us. Joe told a story and he used the word "dago." I'm not sure Eleanor ever really forgave him for that. She just thought, and Alice did too, I'm sure, that Joe was just another one of Blue's ways of defying the family. You could see Alice wince whenever Joe used Blue's name, and I remember at the wedding, which was a great big affair out on the east lawn—Joe's father was there, drunk as a skunk, pulling on the tent ropes—and all Eleanor did was complain about how beautiful the gown was. It *was* a lovely gown, peau de soie, and just an off-white—an Eskimo could tell you—trimmed with lace that Uncle Edwin bought in Brussels. But all Eleanor could talk about the whole day was what a shame it was for such a lovely gown to go to waste.

They never really gave Joe a chance, you know. I lived not so far from them after they moved out to San Diego. They were in a little apartment near the ocean that Joe used to call "Sullivan West," and they were so happy. He was just out of the service, working at one of the radio stations, and Blue was teaching at the university. Her painting had become so important to her, and I think Joe was just the perfect balance. There's something about Joe, and I know it's going to sound odd in retrospect, but I've always thought of him as an honest man. For all his rough and tumble swagger, Joe is actually very simple with his feelings, he's close to his own surface, and I think that's what Blue needed. She couldn't really be bothered with people who didn't make themselves clear, and Joe, the way he'd take her hand in the front seat or bring picnic baskets to the studio she used to work in at the university, Joe made himself very clear.

Blue's father used to have an expression, which I'm going to have trouble remembering. He'd say if people were trees, most of them wouldn't even be honest enough to lean towards the sun. And it's true there aren't many, I think, but Blue found a man who would. She always said Joe leans towards the sun, and I think for her that may have been the most important thing.

Joe Boone

Right after we moved to the house, my father came down from L.A. and set up around ten minutes away. He was getting real old by that time, and he never liked California. He always missed Texas and the things he had down there. He'd been a sheriff for a while in Gilpin. That's where I was born, and Dad kept the peace. Nothing ever made him happier. He was a real charmer. When I was a kid, he used to sit me down on his knee and put his bourbon between my legs and tell me stories, prairie-shit romantic Western stories about horses instead of people, and all I can remember is looking at the hair growing out of his ears. To this day I think about the hair growing out of Dad's ears, and sure enough, you look in the mirror when you hit fifty, and there it is, you got the same damn thing.

Anyway, by the time he came down to San Diego, he was headed downhill. He went through about fifteen different nurses in two years—Blue really had to take over. Every week he'd call up, we'd ask how's your new nurse, and he'd say, I fired her. Blue would just go on up. She'd clean the house, do his sheets, make him roast beef and cucumber sandwiches the way he liked them. There wasn't a Mexican woman alive who could make a sandwich my dad could eat, but Blue's sandwiches were okay.

There were times he'd pretend to forget where he was—I don't know if he was pretending or not—he'd start calling you names like Poonjab or Silver. But you should have seen her, the way Blue handled him. She would take Eton, and he was just a baby still, and she'd give him to Dad and say, "Here, this is your grandson." And when Dad was holding Eton, it didn't seem to matter if he knew who the rest of us were. He'd get it all back. He'd say, "All right, all right. You're Joe."

But Dad knew more than he let on. I think he just liked having Blue around, and any time she did anything, he'd just look at me and shake his head. He even said it to me once. We'd come over for a visit and we were dropping off a portrait Blue had done of him. She'd brought her easel over one afternoon and they'd gone out into the mountains and she'd painted him sitting there in his spurs with his hat. No one else in the world could have made him sit still for it. But anyway, she and I had come over one morning to drop it off. We had to stay and listen to him complain about how all the nurses were stealing things, and right before we left—Blue had gone out already—Dad grabbed me by the arm and he was looking at the painting she'd done, but he meant her. He looked at me and he said, "How the hell did you land that?" I wanted to say, "Dad, I don't know. I have no idea." I felt like the luckiest man in the world.

Claire Sullivan

Blue started bringing Eton into the studio with her in the mornings when he was still very young. The smell of turpentine and oils and paint thinner must have been second nature for him. I know he had a playpen in there for a while, and by the time he was too big for that, he was already painting. She bought him his own brushes and his pads, and from what I could see, he was a natural little artist, with a tiny blue smock and all his mother's painting mannerisms. Blue used to have a black-and-white photograph of Turner in her studio, studying his canvas with his elbow jutting and his hand on his hip with all the brushes sticking out. And sometimes when I'd come in, there'd be Blue intent on her canvas, with her hand under her chin, and then Eton with his hands on his hips and brushes in each. It looked like the three stages of the artist or some such thing.

But I never saw Joe in there, not in the studio at the Lemon House. I think he understood it wasn't his place. I remember asking Blue about a painting once, of sailboats. She'd gone to Monterey on a commission and done a whole series of paintings of sailboats and dinghies, and I knew that Joe hadn't gone with her, but I asked her if he'd seen them yet. She just said, "No, Joe doesn't really look at what I do," and it wasn't out of spite or anger or anything at all bitter. It sounded more like a comfortable agreement they'd had—that her work was separate and something he wouldn't necessarily be able to share in. I think that was one of the wonderful things about Joe, how well he was able to accept the fact that with Blue, there was this other very private realm, and if you weren't invited, then you just had to accept that.

Levi Mottl

I got my first glimpse of San Diego at about three o'clock in the morning, right off the bus. I spent the whole night roaming the streets, and I couldn't get over the quiet, coming from New York. The streets had a swabbed feel. The whole place just looked deserted to me, and it's not an impression I ever really got over, that something was missing. San Diego's always sort of struck me as the town out of a dull person's imagination. I didn't really feel much spirit there until I met Blue.

She was teaching one of the courses in the graduate art program at UCSD, a class in oil painting and color theory. I'd taken some courses at the League in New York, but I still wasn't comfortable with color, and I was looking to Blue's class to help me there. I was anxious to try my hand at the landscape around San Diego. That whole Southern Californian palette sort of swept me off my feet, the clay and purple in the mountains and that cornflower blue—I spent most of my time out in the hills with a canteen and a sketch pad, when I wasn't in class.

It was a while before Blue let us anywhere near landscapes, though. We opened with a lot of still lifes. We were drawing dappled pears one of the first days, a bosc, a red bartlett, and a seckel, probably—Blue was always sort of partial to the seckel. She was making rounds. The first thing she ever said to me was, "Do you see pears?" I nodded. She said, "I don't see pears. I see that," and she sort of waved her hand toward the plate. Her hair was auburn and there was a strand hanging down from a black velvet clip she used to wear for class. She was squinting out, and I remember wanting to see what she was seeing. I just stared at her and I don't know how long, but Blue you could watch sometimes and not even worry, because she'd get a sort of spellbound look in her eye. She could get it cutting a loaf of bread, watching the sky change—the simplest things—but as long as there was a shape and color to it, she'd be drawn in. She'd look, and it's not the way you or I would ever see things. It's not the way things are used to being looked at. I always sort of thought Blue made the world blush, and that's why it looked to her the way it did.

Joe Boone

There were very good years. They're always good years when you're building a family, aren't they? Everything worked. The kids were healthy, Blue was happy at the university. I felt like every day I was coming home to a house that was just sitting on air. A problem? A problem is some fat girl named Zabriskie hits Toddy on the pinky with a rock, or Eton's teachers are complaining that my kid is picking his nose for the other kids. You know, nothing you can't fix with a little ammonia.

And we used to have things we always did, little rituals. Wednesdays we'd take Eton down to the wharf to watch the fishing boats come in, see what they'd caught and pick out a fish, a swordfish, for dinner. We took him to see the battleships. You know, I can show you—we've got pictures of a very good time, of Eton up on my shoulders, all of us out at the opening week at Disneyland, Toddy in his stroller, laughing, the three of us with the mouse ears and Blue shading her eyes.

Levi Mottl

We would go after class to campus coffee shops—under turquoise canopies is where I picture it, with our portfolios leaning up against the third chair. I'd gotten to know her better when some work of mine was selected for a student exhibit up at The Art Center School, and Blue and I and some other students had taken the train up to Los Angeles together. The second semester, Blue had had to stay home for a month when Toddy got the measles, and that's when I started working as a teaching assistant for her classes.

I used to come over to the house, and Blue would take me out to the back yard. She'd stand out there and it was like watching her bloom. There was a lemon tree and the yard wasn't very big. It faced the ocean, just a half mile down the hill, so there was always a light salt in the air. At dusk the clouds would get a sort of salmon color, and shafts of light would spill through the leaves of the lemon tree and shift in the breeze. The house was stucco and Blue would point at the shadows on the white face and say how azure they were, to match the sky. We'd look at how the light would catch the hanging plants, or the shadows of the smoked-glass bottles she used to set out on the ledge. And when the lemons were out in the summer, they'd glint in the twilight. The yellow could just stain your eyes.

Claire Sullivan

I've never known Levi as well as I thought I should have. I think I always agreed with Joe, though. He's such an odd duck I don't think you find yourself wondering whether or not he's a threat. You'd come in and find him occasionally, out in the back yard, feeling the leaves of the tree, or crouching down, kneeling over something in the garden, pulling a worm out of the ground and holding it in his hands for Toddy to look at. He's so thoughtful with everything he does and says—he's so damn slow and steady, like the tortoise—but with those long limbs and wonderful long elegant fingers. And his poor face, that face, you can't help looking at it and thinking about the shape of his marvelous skull underneath, or his Adam's apple. It looked so vulnerable gulping there, like some trapped diamond that Eton used to talk about plucking from Levi's neck with his melon spoon. He'd make Toddy touch it with his finger. Levi would swallow and Toddy would go screaming off down the hall laughing.

Levi Mottl

I was sitting in a sort of semi-dining room that was just off the
living room, and there was a piano. Eton had been playing when
I came in, tinkering. He was around eight. He stopped and asked
if I wanted to play. I'm not much with a piano, but I sat down
and began "Clair de lune," which is one of the few things I can
play with any kind of touch. Eton put his hands over his ears like
so. He closed his eyes and pressed his forehead up against the
piano. I wasn't sure what he was doing. Sometimes I don't really
have much of a feel for children, and I think they know, like
horses. He very slowly pulled the lid down on my fingers to stop
me, and he asked me to play something louder. I consented. One
of the few things I know in forte style is "The Battle Hymn of
the Republic," so I began to play it as a march for Eton. He
pressed himself up against the side of the piano again. I didn't
want to burst his eardrums. I played lightly, but he got up and
he was sort of impatient. He told me to do what he'd been doing,
and *he'd* play. So I got down on my hands and knees and pressed
my ear up against the side of the piano. Eton got up on the bench
and began pounding the bass notes and stretching so he could
floor the sustain pedal. I thought it was a strange sort of attack
at first, but if you got your cheekbone flush and pressed your
head up against the case just right, you could feel the vibrations
trilling through your head. They'd sort of rattle your skull and
you could feel your tongue start to tickle. Eton was just banging
away, pounding the bass and I was down on the floor with my
eyes closed, trying to feel the tickle slipping down my throat. It
stopped suddenly. I looked up at Eton and he'd cocked his head
like a rabbit as if he'd heard something, and very faintly from the
kitchen you could hear Blue, "Shhhhhhhhhhh."

Toddy Boone

I remember pissing contests in the backyard, I remember him running around the house with a towel stuffed in the back of his shirt like a cape, I remember him coming up to me in the hallways at school and pinching my butt. We were brothers. We played. We had this giant pair of pants that had belonged to Grampa—they were even too big for Dad—and Eton and I used to get inside them together and walk around and Dad would pretend that he didn't know where I was. He'd say, "Eton, have you seen Toddy, I've got five hundred dollars for him." And Eton would say, "No, no, Dad, I'll take it." And then I'd stick my hand out of the zipper. Stuff like that, I guess. I remember afternoons at home, in the backyard. We'd just roll around out there for hours, and he'd pin me down and he'd have just drunk a Nehi, and he'd let this gob of spit drip out of his mouth, this long strand, and then suck it back up right before it hit me in the nose.

Joe Boone

Blue and I had a thing we called the Mazatlán lesson. We'd gone down to Mazatlán the spring before Eton was born. Blue must have been five, six months pregnant. She was more than showing, though. Eton was in there kicking away, and as beautiful a thing as all that was to us, you know how women can be. She was a little grouchy. But it's a beautiful place, and I was very happy at the time. We'd taken one of the paddleboats they had. We were out there in the middle of the bay and the sun was coming down, and Blue was looking beautiful the way a healthy mother can. That glow, that full glow. And I guess you could say I was pouring my affection on her, and sure it was hot, but I didn't care. I loved her and I was kissing her to death. But she was all grumpy and hunching up her shoulders. She said it wasn't what she needed right then. Not now.

And I told her something. I let her in on a secret, something I've always known. It's probably one of the things I'm proudest of having shared with Blue. And that was that love, or affection, or whatever you want to call it, well, some people act like it's an arrow, like it's this thing where the timing has to be right and you're doing it for the other person. If they're ready and they're willing, then it turns into a beautiful thing. And that's true—I'm not saying that isn't true—it can be that way.

But there's something else about it too. You know, sometimes love is something you just want to show. You have to let go of it. Maybe she's feeling hot and sticky, maybe this isn't the right time. For her. But it doesn't have to work that way. It's not this arrow that hits or misses. It's this arrow that says, "Hey, I love you whether you want to hear it or not." And you've just got to get it out. Half the time I'd have been happy to just kiss a brick wall and show it to Blue. It feels good to love someone, so do it and show it whenever you want. You don't do it just to make them feel good. You do it for yourself. That's the Mazatlán lesson.

Well, I jump ahead now to a time when Eton must have been eight or nine, somewhere in there. It was a Saturday afternoon, and he was in a terrible mood. He'd gone out on a friend's fishing boat, and he thought he was going to have a nice day fishing, but the kid's father, a real martinet I'd been in the service with, he'd made the boys buff the boat the whole day. I don't even think they got out of the dock. So Eton was storming around, banging around in the kitchen looking for something to drink, and I was trying to calm him down. I told him an embarrassing story about the man, back in the service together—he got beat up by a couple of hookers once in Honolulu. But Eton wasn't even listening he was still so mad.

Blue came in from the studio, and she had turpentine all over her hands, and she hadn't seen Eton all day, because he'd had to get up early for Christ's sake—the son of a bitch had been honking his horn in the driveway at five-thirty in the morning. Anyway, Blue hadn't seen him and went over to him where he was making a chocolate milk or one of his drinks, and he pulled away, you know, "Ma, your hands are all wet." You know, grumpy little boy looking for a shotgun. But she put her hands back on his cheeks. You know, she just wanted to put her hands on his cheeks, and she whispered something in his ear before she went upstairs. And when she'd gone and he'd finished making his milk, Eton looked up at me and said, "Dad, what's the Mazel tov lesson?"

Claire Sullivan

You'll want glimpses. We always look for glimpses, and the one I like to tell is of being upstairs with Blue, reading to Toddy, while Eton had been downstairs drawing. He was ten or so. It was late afternoon and we heard the door slam downstairs and the keys in the dish, all the noises of someone arriving home—the noises of Joe coming home after a rotten, rotten day. The door slams, he trudges into the kitchen, the refrigerator door opens and you could hear the bottles rattling around, and then one placed on the counter, a beer bottle. The pop and hiss of the beer being opened. The rustle of the newspaper. He may have kicked something across the floor, but then the unmistakable sound of Joe Boone's feet coming upstairs, and the change jangling in his pockets.

Now, I really wasn't there a great deal, but you know how you come to know the sound of someone's footsteps, the sound of them banging around a place. And Joe's feet came trudging up the hallway to Toddy's room—thump, thump, thump—and the door swings open, and there stands Eton in one of his father's jackets, with a bottle of beer in his hand and an enormous grin on his face, a very happy grin, almost as if he'd just heard a naughty joke rather than played one. Toddy was just howling with delight, which should tell you something about how accurate it must have been—and that he'd seen these sorts of things before. I don't know how Eton did it. I was just bowled over, all of us were, but Eton sauntered up to me, still smiling, this little ten-year-old boy with the devil in his eye, and he offered me the beer.

He was so delightful, just a delightful little boy, and he could do it on demand, that sort of thing. It was a very strange ability. You'd just catch him doing these sound imitations. He'd do them for Toddy mostly. I can remember them sitting at the dining room table, and Toddy would just start to giggle, because Eton would be doing one of his little tricks. He'd be twirling his fingers in his glass the way Levi used to. He'd have gotten out one of Levi's tall glasses, and he'd put the exact right number of ice cubes in, and just the right amount of iced tea. He fixed it so that it made the very same sound. Toddy and he would both hush up and listen, and Eton would twirl the cubes just so. Then he'd sniffle like Levi and they'd both burst out laughing hysterically again. He liked to do Joe chewing his food too, or reading the paper, folding it just right, smacking it in the middle, digging his finger in his ear and jiggling it the way Joe does. It was all very silly, I know, but I've never known a boy who could be so much fun to be around.

Levi Mottl

I was there four years initially. The last year or so I'd begun to incline towards a lifestyle that wasn't quite as easy to anchor. I went up to Big Sur a number of times in 1958 and spent several weekends that winter in San Francisco, and although I wouldn't say I felt any real desire to become a part of the culture that was taking shape up there, I'd liked the idea of getting out and exploring a little more, casting my line again. The world was starting to seem like something worth going out and seeing a little more of, and I think once I felt that tension in my limbs, the pull of the more nomadic existence, I had to admit to myself that the only thing stapling me put was Blue, and I never wanted to resent her. I just left at the end of the school year. I never spoke to her about any of it. I wrote her five or six drafts of a letter I never sent. I suppose somewhere I felt I'd be returning.

Claire Sullivan

Blue first became sick the winter of 1959. I doubt that there had been a lump there long before she found it. I don't think it shocked her. She had always considered herself almost too lucky a person. She had so many fortunes, and I don't think she really fought misfortune when it came. In an odd way, to her I think it might have seemed ungrateful.

Joe Boone

I came home with abalone one afternoon in December. I found her sitting in the backyard with a straw hat on her head. I remember sneaking up behind her with the abalone in my hand and she turned to me, and she was very pale. Before I could do anything she said she had a lump. For the first time in her whole life she looked scared. I took her right to a doctor, a friend of mine at the base hospital.

And you know, there are certain words in the English language, a word like cancer. It's a mean word. You know, some things it seems like you're waiting your whole life to respond to. There'll be some moment more horrible than anything else, and what'll you do when that moment comes? I wanted to strangle the son of a bitch. Okay, it's cancer, but don't tell me it's malignant. And he calls you in again and says, yes, it's malignant. And you just want to say, for Christ's sake, then cut her breast off. Get it off her. Cut my arm off. Anything.

But there were so many delays, so many tests. It looked like it was going away, but it didn't. It wasn't until the winter that she had her mastectomy, the first one. I don't think we were ever convinced it was all gone.

From RUTH, by Eton Arthur Boone

Dad had passed me an envelope in the kitchen, but I hadn't had much time to ask what it was. I was in seventh grade, and I'd started biking to school in the morning. Sixth graders rode the bus. Seventh graders rode bikes. Those with any social standing tended to ride in packs, and ours was a fairly well-oiled, synchronized operation, able on occasional mornings to get to Juan Cabrillo perfectly intact without braking. It was enough of a thrill when it worked that I used to eat breakfast with my backpack on so I could leave straightaway to hook up with the phalanx at Francis Avenue. Dad's request had been a small hitch. He'd handed me the envelope just as I was stuffing my pants into my socks. He said it was for my substitute teacher, Mrs. Cutter, and he held it out to me with his head turned, as if he'd been asking me to pick a card. I took it and left him at the refrigerator door, sniffing the milk.

He'd seemed out of sorts that morning, right from the start. He'd been different. He'd dressed. Every day since Mom had been at the hospital, he'd come down in his bathrobe, fixed us breakfast, and he didn't get ready for his day until both my brother and I were gone. But that morning when I got downstairs, he'd already showered, shaved, and combed his hair. He'd met me at the breakfast table in a tie and his coat was draped over the kitchen stool. He hadn't said a word until he gave me the note for Mrs. Cutter, and I'd left too soon for him to say anything after.

When I got out to the front lawn with my bike, I looked back in the kitchen window to see if my brother had come down yet. Dad was at the table, sitting with his hands in his lap. He looked like a wax figure in a museum. *The Union* sat at my brother's place, with the rubber band still wound around its waist, and the room was motionless but for the even sweep of the second hand on the wall clock.

I decided not to rap on the window or wave, and that morning I biked past Francis Avenue and took La Cienega into Juan Cabrillo alone.

Claire Sullivan

Blue was an angel about the mastectomy. She was so brave, but she did not fight. I remember seeing her in the hospital after the operation. She'd taken it all so calmly. She'd assured me that it wasn't life-threatening, that they could make a fairly clean cut of

it and that she was actually very fortunate. But a few days after
the operation I visited her and she was lying there, very uncomfortable having to be attended to, lying there so helpless, which
was so un-Blue, and I remember her looking down at herself and
she was in one of those awful smocks that they make you wear.
She had the tag around her wrist and she spoke about her breasts.
"I had a very pretty breast. They were very pretty breasts, don't
you think?"

It wasn't vain, and it didn't sound like her—it sounded like the
voice of a child, so sweet and scared. She lifted her arm very
weakly and touched herself, and I'd never thought about it. All
I could say was the truth, what came into my head, I said, "Yes,
absolutely beautiful," because they were—she was. I said, "You
are absolutely beautiful." And I walked over to her and held her
and I remember I've just never wanted to love someone so much.
She was like a little child there.

Levi Mottl

I'd worked for a number of months in a cannery in Vancouver,
and then I'd gone up to Alaska in March. I'd taken a fishing boat
up from Seattle to Juneau, and then sat in the back of a dump
truck for eleven hours all the way to Anchorage. When I got
there, it was the first time I called San Diego since I'd been away.

It's funny. I'd been so exhilarated, placing my call from the
back room of a truck stop just inside the city limit, a place run
by an authentic Aleutian named Dolly, and with a sunset so early
in the afternoon. Everything had struck me as so extraordinary
and wide, but when Joe told me, it was a bitter feeling in my
stomach, a feeling that sort of had teeth. I felt deprived. That
night I spent outdoors, watching the stars move more slowly than
I'd ever been accustomed to seeing them, and thinking about her.
Not about Blue in the hospital, but the Blue I'd first known.

It was an afternoon. I'd come in a little early and I'd just been
waiting in the living room. There was a bathroom down that way,
down a tiled hallway—of hacienda tiles. I could hear Blue in there
giving Toddy a bath. He couldn't have been more than three and

the wallpaper downstairs had wheels on it. I'd waited, made myself at home. I'd begun watering some of the plants, some fuchsia that used to hang by the sliding doors, and a baby palm. I was watering them when Toddy came running down the hallway laughing, and she followed him with towels. Both of them were soaking wet and neither of them had anything on. He ran right up to me. I caught him at my thigh, and she was three feet away, dripping on the tiles. I just stood there, with a tin watering pail in my hand, and with Toddy drying himself on my pant leg. It didn't last long. She covered herself, but there was an expression on her face I think I might have misunderstood, as if it had been casual, as if seeing her hadn't mattered. I didn't think it had.

And I suppose what I was feeling that night in Anchorage, passing a pipe with the man who'd driven the dump truck from Juneau, a man named Harvey or Charley whose brother was in jail, I was wondering to myself if this is what it took to see it did matter, that Blue's body had to be cut open. I know they tell you that you can't go home again, and I suppose I'd always thought that was because you change, but no one had ever told me that sometimes the reason you can't go home is because it's been ransacked.

From RUTH, by Eton Arthur Boone

I didn't see Mrs. Cutter again until the following week, after the second operation. I used to play in the upstairs hallway with an oversized yellow marble, wood blocks, and magazines. My brother and I would create whole courses with the blocks and pillows and weeklies, and the marble could follow only if it was rolled correctly, with just the right speed and spin. Most of the time it was distracted by the pitch of the hallway, which leaned south, down toward the living room. The whole house slumped in toward its center, so that if you lifted all its dividing walls and placed marbles at all its corners, they'd converge under the living room table, which was a big bronze platter on legs. They'd all roll and pat Homer softly on her belly as she slept, as if she'd swallowed a magnet for marbles.

Life and *The Saturday Evening Post* had the best surfaces for marbles, but they were kept on a rack in my father's den, and I didn't like to go in there in the afternoons, because when my father wasn't home and the shutters were closed, the den always seemed asleep to me, faint and airless. It was only 2:30. I was home early because Hector's birthday party had been called off. His mother's appendix had burst that afternoon, and I couldn't imagine that anyone would be home, because my brother would still be at Vega's All Stars, and my father had been taking his lunches at the hospital.

I crept toward the door of his den regardless and found it ajar. When I peered through the crack I saw my father kneeling between Mrs. Cutter's knees. Her skirt was hiked up. Her thighs were spread to welcome his chest, and her shirt was open, breasts bared for my father's frantic suckling. Mrs. Cutter's head was thrown back in an embarrassed ecstasy and her fingers rummaged awkwardly through my father's hair as he poured over her. I didn't stay long in the door frame, only long enough to see a single grind of Mrs. Cutter's full hips buck my father's head and upset his feast like a ground swell. Long enough to hear the slavish moans of two people who'd been beaten and to see her thighs close in on him more gracefully and her ankles hook and rub themselves, the way you'd imagine horses or swans necking. I slowly stepped back and out of sight. I didn't pull the door with me. I could feel my face flush and gave in to the pull of the house's center under the living room table, where Homer must have swallowed a magnet for shame.

Joe Boone

I don't know why. Something turns off inside. You stop thinking. You start just doing things because they're there. I just felt so damn alone, I think I'd have done anything to feel like it wasn't happening. When Blue got sick—I mean, I don't want to say this, because I loved Blue and I don't need to explain that to anyone, but Christ, how do you take care of a woman like that? She just pulled back. She acted like it was no one's business. I'd wake up and find her in the bathroom downstairs, sick and her whole body shaking, and I'd say, Blue, wake me up, but she never would. It was like she just took it in, you know. She accepted it, she moved on. And I couldn't do that. I panicked. I made a horrible, horrible mistake. But there's some things where you've just got to say, it happened. I can't do anything about it.

It's the part with Eton, I still don't know. I think I just wanted to have something with him. Because he'd just taken it in like Blue. He was like this little engine that just keeps going. He never cried. I'd go in his room at night to tuck him in. I'd ask how he was doing and he'd ask me medical questions. I just wanted us to have each other, see what we were going through—you know, not exactly, there's such a thing as fathers and sons—but I just wanted to grab him sometimes and say, "Okay, we should adjust. You're right. If there's a flood, you look for something that floats, I know, but it's still okay to stop for a second. It's okay to say, 'This stinks,' Eton. It's okay to know that people need help, that they can't do everything alone." And if he can see that—that we're not going to be heroes in front of this thing, this thing just beats us—well, then maybe it isn't the worst thing in the world.

I'm not saying it was the right thing to do. I'm not saying that at all. It was horrible and I'm going to have to live with it for the rest of my life. But I remember the second time, and this is not in the book. He was leaving to go, and I'd caught him on the stairs. I'd wrestled with it, but I saw him going. You go ahead and do something when it's wrecking you like that. I just gave him the note, Eton, could you do this for me? And he just looked at me. He reached out and took it on the stairs and put it in his bag. And I couldn't let him go just like that. I mean, I was trying to get through to him. I put my hand on his shoulder to say, you know, whatever, son, we're here together, aren't we? Thank him for that, and show him there was something strong about it. I wasn't looking for comfort. I wasn't looking for someone to tell me it was okay. Don't let people tell you that. Don't let people tell you that's what I needed. Eton knew what I needed, and he just looked at me to say, yes, he knew, I swear he did, and then he left.

Toddy Boone

Dad took me on a fishing trip, just four days up near Mount Palomar while Mom and Eton were in the Southwest. I know I was thinking that somewhere down the road we'd switch up. Mom would take me to the Southwest, and Dad would take Eton fishing.

I don't really remember what kind of fish it was that we were up there trying to catch, but I remember we'd gotten the wrong bait. We'd stopped off at a tackle and bait shop on the way up, and Dad said we'd been given a bum steer by the man up there. That was the first time I heard the expression "bum steer." And the night after our first day fishing, I said to Dad as he was tucking me in—we used to have a little ritual where I would have to tell him every night one thing that I'd learned that day—and I told him I'd learned that we'd gotten a bum steer and he should remember for when Eton came up not to go to that tackle and bait shop. But Dad said, "Eton's not coming up here. This place is yours and mine." And I knew he was trying to make me feel good, but I also knew it meant that New Mexico and Arizona belonged to Mom and Eton. That's probably when I realized things weren't exactly even Steven.

From RUTH, by Eton Arthur Boone

Santa Fe came as a relief to us both. I think the Southwestern landscape had worn our patience for shades of muddy pink and copper. I'd enjoyed our roughing days most during twilight and early morning, when lights and colors aren't reflections so much as the seeping of every surface, when each rock or strip of sky is a lamp shaded blue or orange. I think I learned most from these times of day because they convinced me that light doesn't play favorites.

I also learned that from my mother's palette. We were painting a landscape just outside of Magdalena, New Mexico. She was on a stool and I was sitting on the back door of the station wagon. It was twilight. I remember painting the landscape as it would appear in the brilliance of day and then shading my picture with what I thought was the grey of twilight. It's funny how a little boy can think shadows are grey when they so rarely are. When I was very young, I once asked my mother about the color of shadows and she told me that a shadow can be just about any color, but I said no. I said they were grey, grey cast on the color of a surface.

Outside Magdalena my mother won the argument with hardly a word, because she was able to find the colors of twilight with no strategy for shading. She saw the glowing copper on the face of a cliff and painted it. She saw the Dodger blue of the sky high above the horizon and found it on her palette. I saw a day washed grey and brown by twilight and I painted mud.

When it became too dark she walked back to the car and saw my painting and said, "There's really not so much grey as you think." She might as well have said there are no such things as shadows at all, just different slabs of color.

Claire Sullivan

Blue was very happy when they returned from New Mexico. I had lunch with her downtown not so long after, in a diner near the radio station. She looked well—I really thought the trip had done wonders for her—and she spoke about Eton. She was so proud of him. She said that Eton was painting better than she was, but she also mentioned she thought he was beginning to drift away from her, naturally, she said. I remember her telling me that it was something all mothers have to come to terms with. But you could just see, if she hadn't had to be at the hospital so much, if she'd seen him when she wasn't there, she might have wondered if it wasn't something more than just a boy growing up. It's so difficult to say after *Ruth.* I don't really know if I'm letting that book color what I remember. But I just hate to think that maybe Eton wasn't drifting at all. Maybe it was a different kind of silence she was hearing, the silence that protects, that hides. It absolutely crushes me to think about how painful it must have been for such a young boy to go off on that trip having to hide such secrets from his mother. That was Joe Boone's real sin. My God, intruding on that wonderful, loving silence between those two—the comfortable silence of painting the same landscape with someone you love—destroying that, that was Joe's real sin.

From RUTH, by Eton Arthur Boone

We were staying at the Terminal Motel, which we thought was a funny name. The Terminal was owned by a woman who looked either Indian or Mexican to me. The sun had baked her race away and she was just old. She sat at the front desk of the motel with an infant in her lap the whole while we were there, and I remember our second evening, when my mother and I were headed out for dinner at a place across the road called The Taco Pit. My mother stopped at the desk to drop off the key and asked, "Es su nieto?"

"No, no," the woman said, smiling and rocking slowly. "Dis my little boy Garcia, my son." She leaned over the boy and rubbed her nose against his. "Si, mi hijo." The baby reached out stiffly and turned its head toward her belly.

"Su hijo?" my mother said. "That's incredible."

The woman looked up and smiled a toothless smile. "Mi sisteen children." She lifted the boy up to my mother.

"That's amazing." My mother took the child in her arms. "Que mujer." She looked down at the boy with a mother's longing. "Your mother is quite a woman. Si, yes." The baby began to squirm and was turning in my mother's cradle, stretching his whole body toward her. She offered me the baby but he was tugging at the silver chain around her neck. She stuck her finger in his tiny palm and began rocking him. "Look at his ears. They look like little shells, don't they?" I stood on my toes and looked over at him as he continued to wriggle in her arms and reach between the buttons of her shirt.

"No, Garcia." The old woman stood up from the desk.

"It's all right," my mother said weakly. The child strained his neck to reach for her, opening its mouth like a baby bird in its nest. And while the little boy groped for my mother I felt as never before that she was mine and would never be anyone else's again.

Toddy Boone

Dad calls it "that bad time." He just sort of lumps all those years together. When I was about twelve, I started wanting to know what the exact order had been, you know, when she'd first gotten sick, when the operations were, when Anne had started coming around, but Dad would just wave it off, he didn't want to talk about it. Eton knew. I was watching TV with him once up in my room—Dad had gotten us this TV that we used to roll into my room on Tuesday nights so I could watch "The Fugitive" and then go right to sleep. Eton and I were up there and I'd asked him if he remembered how it had worked exactly. He turned down the volume and just reeled off the facts.

It was almost exactly two years, according to him. She'd first gotten sick in late '59, the first operations were the following spring. Their trip was June of '60. She did okay from then until the winter and then she had uterine lumps—that's early, early '61. She was in and out of the hospital the whole last year, and that was the summer—again, this is according to Eton, but I think he was the only one really keeping track—but that was the summer Anne started helping out. Eton called her "Blanne." I probably first saw her right at the end of third grade. She brought me coloring books of "Bonanza."

Anne Richman Boone

I met Joe at a children's birthday party which both Toddy and Hilary went to. It was the summer. Hilary didn't get to be in San Diego very much, so he didn't have very many friends here, but my boss's nephew was having a party at the zoo, and I was able to get Hilary to go. It wasn't easy finding friends for Hilary, because of prejudice. I think Hilary had to face a lot of that. It's one thing to confront prejudice on your own as I did with Hilary's father Damon, but it's another thing to be the child of a mixed marriage. That's part of the reason I kept Hilary in boarding school after the divorce—at least they accepted him there as part of the community.

But little boys need friends, and in San Diego, Toddy was one of the first boys to play with Hilary. They'd first met at this birthday party at the zoo, and Joe and I had come to pick them up. The boys were in the same station wagon coming back, and Joe and I talked while we were waiting. Joe was so nice. I thought, what a wonderful sweet man, and what a horrible burden for him to have to shoulder. And he was there before any of the other parents, with a sweater for Toddy. And when the boys arrived, we saw they were in the back seat together, and Hilary looked like he'd been crying, and I think Toddy was the only little boy who would talk to him at all. Toddy was a very sweet little boy. They came up to us, and Hilary had cotton candy all over his clothes, and Joe said, well, let's have everyone over for dinner tonight and get everyone scrubbed up. I don't even think he thought twice about it.

Claire Sullivan

I visited Blue as often as I could, at least two or three times a week, but she actually told me that I might do better to set her mind at ease if I could stop by the house and see that things were running smoothly there, maybe fix the boys a real meal. Well, I did. I stopped by occasionally to see what I could do, maybe make a meatloaf or a casserole, things that keep.

But one afternoon I dropped by with some groceries and found a woman in the kitchen making a pie. She was very nice, really about as pleasant a thing as you can find in a kitchen. But it was a rather awkward conversation because I didn't know if she was there on a paying basis. She didn't look like someone you'd pay for. She was a very attractive package, with good, simple looks.

She struck me as looking like a blond Jackie Kennedy. Slim. She had on a pearl necklace. The only thing that was curious about her was how comfortable she seemed to be in that kitchen. Maybe that's why she seemed a little professional to me. But she said no, she said that she was just there to help Joe and the boys. She said, you know, we all have to pull together in times like these, and she'd sort of cocked her head when she said it, sitting at the kitchen table with her hands in her lap, and I remember thinking to myself that either here was the most gracious and kind woman on God's earth, or a madwoman had found her way into Blue's kitchen.

So the next time I was at the hospital, I had this very delicate piece of news for Blue, that there was a kindly apparition baking pies in her oven. I don't think that Blue had met Anne yet—in fact I'm certain she hadn't—but she gestured to calm me. She said, "Yes, that must be Anne Richman. Joe tells me he's found an angel to help out when she can."

Joe Boone

Lumps on her throat, in her neck. Back and forth for the tests and those damn vitamins. It's all just a blur. The truth is, the doctors, they didn't know what the hell was going on. And we didn't know how much to tell the kids—Do you tell Eton? How much can Toddy know? It seemed like it was all Blue and I got to talk about anymore. I hated all that damn strategy. I hated that every time I talked to Eton, it was just to tell him that she was getting worse, that it was probably just a matter of time.

Toddy Boone

I saw Mom and Eton dancing once. I wasn't in the room. I was looking in, into the living room where the record player was, and Mom was teaching him to ballroom dance. It was in the middle of the day. We had giant glass doors that opened out to the backyard, and the sun used to come in in the afternoon. Eton and Mom were just like silhouettes against the sliding doors, and they were laughing. It actually kind of scared me to see her up like that because I'd thought she was too sick, but she was laughing. They were stepping on each other's toes, and he was holding her, just rocking back and forth. I wish I could remember what they were dancing to. Someone like Nat "King" Cole. I don't remember. I just watched them, holding my breath. I'd remember it if I heard it.

Levi Mottl

I didn't think I should go back to San Diego. I was living in Saskatchewan, assisting at a school for the deaf there, and it hadn't been easy. I'd wake up at around six every morning and walk four miles to school, watching the sun rise. I'd watch the pink and ochre wash out the windsor blue, and think about Blue back in the hospital. I'd spoken to her a couple of times, but mostly to Joe. It didn't seem like she'd broken free of the hospital, but I couldn't imagine her being sick. I'd think about sending her some bottles of dusk in a box, to shine on her wall when the nurses weren't looking.

But Joe called after the hysterectomy. He said the doctors didn't think Blue was going to be getting any better, and he thought someone should be there for Eton. Joe said he felt like he'd lost him, and he asked if I'd come back.

I guess at the time I assumed Joe was just being a champ, giving me an excuse to return. I think to an extent that's probably true, but it was also true that Eton was in a shell. It wasn't hard to see why, the change in Blue was so dramatic. She looked completely different, sort of gutted. I don't think I could have imagined it, Blue shuffling across the floor, her hair so thin, her arms spotted and all the color gone from her face. The drugs she was on, it seemed like she'd retired from life, and I suppose I found it a little more stunning than I could take with any kind of grace or strength. I couldn't blame Eton for closing off.

We would go to the hospital together. I remember at the end of one of our visits, Blue's face. She'd tried to hold his hand while he was by the bed and all he'd said was it felt waxy. As he left the room she'd looked over at the wall and her eyes filled. I think it was for Eton she feared death most. She didn't want it because of him, and she looked at the wall and waited to be left alone. Before I left, she said, "Please tell him it's fine."

I drove back with Eton next to me in the front, silent and staring straight ahead. We drove out to the coast, but before we reached the highway he asked me to stop the car and he got out, and he got in the back, and we drove off again. I didn't take him home. We drove up along the coast, and he laid down in the back seat crying.

Anne Richman Boone

Once a week I would go do a shopping for them all, and this was one of the first times I had done it. I had all the bags out on the kitchen counter, and I remember I was putting the things away in the cupboards when I saw Eton ride up on his bicycle. And, you know, I felt awkward about being in the kitchen, alone in the house with no one else. So I got myself ready for him. I straightened my skirt and dried my hands. I got ready to welcome him and offer a sandwich or something to drink. I remember I'd even taken down a glass from the cupboard, and I'd poured an apple juice for him. And I just waited for him. I listened for the sound of the door. And I waited, and I listened, and I waited. And I waited some more until I started to ask myself had I really seen him. I was sure it was him, though. I'd seen him through the window, and he'd seen me. But he didn't come.

So I sat there, and I couldn't just leave all the bags out, so I put the rest of the things away as quickly as I could. I'd bought some things for lunch. I made him a baloney sandwich and put it on a dish in the ice box for him, next to the glass of apple juice. I just felt so awful. I went out the back door.

Levi Mottl

Blue reached out and took my hand one day in the hospital room very near the end. It was just the two of us, and she didn't say a word for a while, for a long time. Then she asked me to open the shades. The sun was streaming in, and there were roses on the windowsill from Joe, red roses, and her voice was very faint, hardly anything at all, and she said, "Look at them," and began to trace the roses with her finger. I put my head very near hers to see them from her angle. Our faces were very close. I could feel the warmth, and you could smell her sickness. She was having a great deal of trouble describing what she saw. She hadn't the breath for complete thoughts, and there was a thick, pale film across her eyes. Finally she managed to ask me what color I thought the flowers were, and the sun was flooding them. They looked red. I said, "Red. Rose red." And she said, she whispered in my ear, like the saddest joke, "Looks aubergine to me."

Claire Sullivan

She died on a gray, hazy day in late December, December 21, 1961. There's something very forgiving about the way someone finally dies after such a long, slow trial. The person leaves the body before the life does. We didn't lose Blue the instant she died—we lost her before.

I was there. I came in every morning, and the last few days she was somewhere in between. I read poems to her, poems that she'd liked best—Blake and Auden—but she was less and less Blue. Her face and her hair and her body, all settling for death. Her cheeks and mouth just lay there on her bones. Blue was gone and death had settled in, but it wasn't so horrifying. It seems right somehow, it happens so gradually but so distinctly. Death really does lay claim to you, and it's the same expression for everyone I've seen. Peace, and not at all the peace of the particular person. The person, your friend, your cousin is gone.

The last day, the last morning I came in, the smell in the room was entirely different. I knew that it was her last. I called Joe, who was still at home making breakfast for the boys, and told him to come down, that she was dying today. He asked me if he should bring the boys, and I've always been sorry for my answer, which I think was too abrupt. I said, "Not to see Blue. Blue is gone." But I'd been touched by Joe there. When he asked, I could see the side of him that makes him a wonderful man, such a really kind man. Because he was helpless. He wanted so much to do the right thing, but he didn't know what that was, and he wasn't at all ashamed to admit it.

He did something odd, though. He brought Eton. He left Toddy with Anne and brought Eton to see her, which mustn't have been easy. I think he must have thought that was the right thing to do. It may have been. I don't know. I was glad Eton was there. He walked right up to her, next to the bed, and he leaned over her. I think he wanted to kiss her goodbye, but he didn't. I think he knew he was too late. He didn't say anything. None of us did, until Joe. He said, "She loved you, you know, Eton. And that's something." Eton didn't respond, didn't even move. But I think that was the right thing.

From RUTH, by Eton Arthur Boone

The Terminal's only soda machine was in the registration office, which was a walk. Our room and the office were at opposite ends of the Terminal's L, but it was a clear evening. The air was cooling, and as I walked along the motel porch the ridge of the Black Range mountains looked like paper cutouts against the lavender sky. They looked flat, and I stared at them to see if the mountains would slide in front of each other like playing cards.

The desk was kept at night by an older man named Jimmy who

was bent and skeletal and whose teeth dangled off his gums like kernels of rotten corn. Jimmy was friendly to me. He broke my dollar and showed me where they kept the ice chest, in a room behind the office. I went in and began chopping myself some ice when I heard the jangle of the door and a couple walk in. They were drunk, and they needed a place. "Do you have rates for half-nights?" the man asked, and I heard the woman laugh. I wanted to see them, but most of the ice in the chest had melted into a single chunk, and I was having trouble chopping it. I had about a quarter-inch of what looked like a shattered windshield in the bucket when I went back in the office.

The man had on a white straw hat and a cream linen suit. His skin was burnt pink, and his eyes looked like olive pits covered in spit. They were dastardly eyes and they nudged both me and Jimmy in the ribs at the prospect of the woman tugging at his jacket. She was more native, with long black hair and smoother skin, skin pulled tight around her bones, except for her breasts, which swayed like water balloons filled to the nipple with liquor. Her nails dug in his jacket fiercely. She had their room key in her free hand, and as the man signed the registration, she traced a white spiral on his cheek with the tip of the key. Just as she was reaching its center, she looked at me out of the corner of her eye, flicked out her tongue and licked a three-inch trail up his neck and into his ear. She dropped the key in his pocket.

The man shucked her aside and she stumbled backwards, pulling up the straps of her dress like the cords of a grocery bag, to keep the fruit from tumbling out. She weaved over to the Coke machine, rummaged around in her purse, inserted a couple of dimes, and without looking at me, said, "Is that ice for your girl, little boy?" I said, "No, it's for the drink." She smiled and opened the glass door, pulled the last Coke from its slot, and turned toward me. For the first time I saw her completely, every drunken lap and swell. She said, "Well, I hope you didn't want a Coke." The man in the white hat snapped his fingers twice and dangled the key out in front of her. She turned back around and her body swished out of the office after him.

Jimmy gave a soft tongue whistle as the door clanged shut. He turned to me and said he was sorry. He called me fella and asked if I'd gotten all the ice I wanted. I said, yeah, and looked over at the soda machine with what must have been visible longing, because he told me there was a store about half a mile down the road, if I had my heart set on a Coke. I thought I did, and my mother was resting in our room. I didn't like being in the room when she was resting because it made me worry. So I had Jimmy point me in the right direction and started toward the road with the bucket of ice still in my hand.

By the time I'd made my way out to the edge of the road, the number 17 had me in its grip. I'd seen it in Jimmy's ledger, the room he'd given them. In room 17, that woman's dress would be slipping to the floor. She'd step out of it and open her mouth on his, slice off his buttons with her nails. The image pulsed in my brain like a slow strobe, a throb of blood, a blinking conscience that would rather see the deep blush of shame on its inside lid than that man and woman together.

She tugged at me, though. She kept leading me, to more and more doors, more sheets, more veils, more dresses slipping from her body, but only just slipping. I could not in my mind have had that woman completely for even a moment, but it made the image no less clear, of her stepping out of that dress and moving towards him. My blood rushed, and it raged with envy for the man, the one who got to go behind the doors with the woman, the one who folded down the sheets and accepted the body as it slipped out of the white dress. If I could somehow be a man, and have her carve spirals in my cheek. If I could have her come to me without questions, without suspicion, with nothing but desire, I would have done anything. I knew the lure of desire almost completely, and I felt in my knees and throat an ache to give in, to let it have me. And just as frightening and vivid to me was the longing with which desire wants a voice, wants to announce and proclaim itself like conviction, or like guilt.

It said, "If you want it, it means something. You need something, and there's no shame in that."

I turned around from the road and walked back toward the wooden stairs of the hotel porch. My steps were slow and tentative, but quiet like Indians as I walked along the planking, and the voice was very clear.

"All you've really got is what you want, and you can walk through your life pretending it isn't there, or that it'll go away, but you'll just drive yourself crazy. You're just a human being. Don't forget that. Wanting is what it's all about."

I stopped outside room 17 and stood profile in front of the window. The curtains were drawn and I could only see the figures in the room very faintly. I could hear their voices. The woman floated into the bathroom and the man was down on the bed waiting. He sensed me outside. He sat up and threw change at the window. I walked on as if I hadn't stopped.

"It's not going to leave you alone. Long as you want something, it's going to be there waiting. You try to push it away like you know better, like you don't need anything, but what you don't know is that's who you are. What you need, that's who you are, and somewhere you've just got to say, 'Okay, then, let's see it.' "

I keyed the door to our room as quietly as I could and pushed it open. I could see my mother's stomach rising and falling slowly with sleep. Her hands were over her belly and her shoes were on. I pulled the door closed and put the bucket down. I looked at my mother. I looked at her chin and her shoulders, her whole body lying there. I crept on flat heels into the bathroom.

The woman was returning to him now from the bathroom, with nothing on, with nothing. Her breasts floated and they were large and white. She smiled and slid onto the bed.

I locked the door and sat on the toilet. My mother didn't stir.

"It doesn't mean that all the other things don't matter. All it means is you're human. All it means is there's a difference between now and everything else, and right now there's something you want."

I was hard. I stretched my legs out and put my foot up against the bathroom door. My pants were straining, taut down around my ankles.

The woman knelt over him, straddled him, with her thighs spread muscularly, and unbuttoned him slowly. Her breasts hovered. They were heavy.

My mother lay still and I held myself in the bathroom, hard up past my belly button.

"And when it gets up close, right there in front of you, that's when you know you're alive. With everything else you'd never know. But having something right there waiting, saying, 'Come on. Come on, give in,' you don't give in, you go. You make that decision and that's the one moment in your life you know you're there. It's just, 'I'm getting that. I'm going.' "

I pulled once, and then twice.

The woman pulled him out of his zipper and held it in her hand like a bottle.

My mother's stomach rose and then fell. Her feet crossed.

I came, for the first time. It smacked my face and plupped against the wall behind me.

I hated him. I hated him. I hated him.

Levi Mottl

The funeral reception was at the Lemon House. It wasn't a big affair. The family. Some from back East. Some students from the school. Anne had prepared the place very competently. She'd made deviled eggs and placed them in a very neat circle around a dip for cauliflower and broccoli. It was a pretty attractive plate, and up until then, I'd liked deviled eggs a great deal.

But I remember I'd gone upstairs to help Toddy with a train set that someone had brought over for him. He was sitting on his bed in a jacket and tie reading the instructions, and I was down on the floor forcing the tracks together, when I heard a voice from the landing, a voice I couldn't quite place. I could just hear it calling out softly, with that knotted, thick throat that's like cloth, calling out, "Mom, Mom." It sounded like Eton, sounding lost, and I'd wanted to let it pass. I just kept on wrestling with the tracks and Toddy was still reading, but I heard the feet coming up the stairs further, and then he called out again, closer to the door, "Mom?" I put down the tracks. I stood up and went to the door. I opened it and there was a little boy standing there in gray flannel shorts and a white button-down. It was one of Alice's children, Blue's sister, and he couldn't have been more than seven, and he said, "Have you seen my mother?" I remember feeling I was going to vomit on the top of his head.

Joe Boone

I wasn't even seeing straight. You know, it seems like there'd been time, she'd been sick for so long, but you just can't prepare for something like that. It's still overnight. We turned from being this family—just because she'd been there—into this man and two boys, and how was that supposed to work? I tried. Jesus, I tried, but the three of us would go out together, just go see a movie, and Toddy said it right. We were driving back from seeing *The Music Man* and he just started crying. He said with the three of us together all it made him think was, "Where's Mom? Why isn't she here?" And I wanted to say, "Toddy, boy, this is it, from now on. This is what we got. We got to get used to it," but I just couldn't. I agreed with him. And we never got used to it. Driving in the car sometimes, right afterwards, I'd look at Eton in the rearview mirror—I feel like it's the only time we looked at each other back then—he's got his arms crossed and I can see it in his eyes. I don't blame him for it, it's natural and I don't blame him, but sitting there in the back seat, I know Eton's thinking, "I wish it had been you, Dad. You should have been the one."

Claire Sullivan

Four years. Four long years. I was just ducking my head in, but it seems to me that Joe spent the first year after she died simply working his fingers to the bone. I actually don't know if it was work that he was doing to pass the time—he may have been driving up and down the coast, for all any of us knew—but he certainly wasn't keeping up with the friends he'd had with Blue. Just holed himself up, didn't even return phone calls. He'd hired a housekeeper named Mrs. Milligan who I don't think any of them had particularly warm feelings towards. A great big Irish woman, she kept the place running, saw to Toddy, which is what it seems to me Anne should have been doing if things had been allowed to run their natural course. But Anne was a little frightened off by Eton, I think. It was very clearly Eton. He hadn't been gone for two months before Joe and Anne were officially engaged. Four years of them all moping about, dipping their toes in the bathwater to see if it's getting any warmer, and then the moment Eton left for Europe, everyone hopped right in. He must have been quite a little black cloud.

Levi Mottl

I stayed six months or so after Blue died, working at the University and checking on Eton. We'd take trips up the coast when we could, day trips, overnights on weekends up Highway 1. We explored, sort of painted the cordial white line between ourselves and everything else that was going on out there. We'd head out to the hills by San Bervasa where they have the red snakes, or go out on the fishing boats off Port Norma, and we had a good time together. Eton and I were a good match. It isn't that you need the same politics or sense of humor as your traveling partner. It doesn't even matter if he's half your age as long as he goes at your pace, and Eton did. That may have been an adjustment he was just naturally able to make, to find your gear, but the time we spent together back then, we gave each other the kind of company you get from a car radio. There. Soothing just for being there, ready to light, ready to tune into.

I'm not sure it was the best thing for Eton, though. I think coming and going like that, using the house as a sort of pit stop, probably just made Eton even more reluctant to be there in the first place. The way he'd get to his room when I'd bring him home—I'd drop him off, but he wouldn't use the front door if Joe's car was in the driveway. If he saw Joe's car, he'd go up to it, get up on the hood, and swing himself up on to the roof by the basketball rim. Then he'd walk across the garage roof to his window. I'd get out of the car to go say hi to Joe, and usually by the time he answered the bell, you could hear Eton's window slam shut.

I left in the middle of the summer, 1962, but before I did I made an offer. I told Joe I could take Eton on a trip after he graduated from high school, to Europe. It was a way of making sure that Eton and I would stay in touch, which I think we wanted to. I guess I also always felt a debt, learning from Blue and knowing her as I did, I had to keep a promise to be sure Eton always knew there was this special take on the world that had belonged to his mother. Joe knew it too. I think I always had his blessing there. So we sort of set this date, Eton and I, to go to Europe together after he graduated, and pick up there.

Toddy Boone

Eton used to take me out to dinner at this place just called Lunch-Annette, maybe once a week, just me and him. He'd take the car. He was too young for his license, but Dad never said anything. I have no idea if Dad remembers this, but he came into Eton's room with a ten dollar bill one time, and he said he'd pay if Eton would take me and Hilary out to Lunch-Annette, because it was Hilary's birthday and he was in from school. Eton just looked at Dad and I remember him saying, "Who the hell is Hilary?" He knew, I think he just wanted to hear Dad say it, Anne's son. Could he please just take Anne's son out for a birthday dinner? We didn't. Eton said no. He didn't even look at him.

Dad ended up taking us, just Hilary and me and Anne. We went to the restaurant in the Coronado, special treat. We'd gone in all dressed up, Hilary was in his uniform. People were staring at him the second he came in. It's like we'd brought in a freak. Halfway through dinner he said he was feeling sick. He just sat there with his chin on his plate. I remember the three of us singing happy birthday to him while the waiter brought out the cake, and no one else joined in. They all just sat there at their tables, clearing their throats.

Hilary Richman

I was born in Bethesda, which is an awful place. I went to grade school, I went to public school there till I was in the middle of second grade. Then this unfortunate incident happened and my parents moved me to a military school, which is where I was until my parents divorced, after we'd moved to California.

Actually it was funny. It's a racial incident, which I recount with glee. I was in second grade and it was at a Christmas party. First of all, we lived on the base, so the school had a lot of military children, and there was this grotesque little boy who was fat and his father was a general or something. He was just horrid. At the Christmas party we had hot chocolate and he was drinking a little mug. He said, "This chocolate is just the color of your skin, you cocoa face" or something like that. I looked over at his hot chocolate and took it and I threw it at him. He was hospitalized. It wasn't boiling—apparently it was very hot, I don't know. So they asked my parents to move me to a different school, which they did. The worst part of it was I had to write a letter to the little shit, apologizing. I'm sure he's in the service now.

Claire Sullivan

Hilary was an adorable child truly, an adorable little brat. I never saw him that much, and when I did, I doubt I was in the best of moods. This was when Blue was really quite ill. He'd come down from his school on vacations, and occasionally he'd come over with Anne to help make something. A very delicate little tawny boy with the most beautiful face, I can see him in Blue's kitchen peering about and watching us all chop up vegetables and such things. And occasionally you'd glance over at him. He was a boy but he still stared like a baby, so unafraid, and like some very dear babies, when you caught him staring he'd give you his wonderful little smile. He must have been very uncomfortable in those situations, and I imagine anywhere he went, because he was so extraordinary. This lovely little boy tiptoeing about the kitchen with his roll of apricot candy.

Oh, but he had the foulest habit with it too. He used to have those rolls, those fruit rolls that are just sheets of dried apricots or some such thing that Anne used to make, and he had one in the kitchen one morning. I was in there starting a ratatouille, and he'd come in the way anyone's bound to when they hear someone fumbling about in the kitchen. He'd taken one of these new rolls, and he was standing right next to me, and he opened it and unrolled it like so and laid it out flat on the counter. And then he brought it up to his face and licked it, he licked it all over. And he was peering out of the corner of his eye as he did so, gleefully. He proceeded to roll it back up. Well, I looked over at him and I said, "Hilary, what on earth are you doing?" And he said, "I'm licking it." He said, "I'm licking it so that if anyone else wants one, this is the one that I've licked. Would you tell the others?" Would I? I felt rather obliged to.

Joe Boone

There was a weekend, a Friday night, and the kids weren't around. Claire had taken them up to Los Angeles, and I'd called Anne. They were having a carnival down by the wharf, and I asked Anne if she'd like to come with me. We'd gone places together before, just the two of us. We'd go on walks down by Imperial and talk. She told me about Damon and all that, how rough it had been. But there was something different about this night, I think Anne felt it too. She looked terrific. Had her hair up. We'd gone down in the early evening and just walked through. They'd set up some fish stands. We danced. They had a mariachi band set up in the square, and we danced. Her hair looked like gold, and we walked up and down the wharf, up and down, dancing to all the different bands they had.

But I'd had to go back to the car. It got dark and it was getting cold, so I'd gone back to get us sweaters. I sat in the car for about ten minutes, just sitting there. And then I went back to the wharf. It looked beautiful at night. All the people, and the lights hanging, streamers, piñatas. It was like being a kid again, and I saw Anne sitting on one of the tables, with just the red checker tablecloth. She had her elbows on her knees and a paper cup in her hand, and she was nodding to people when they came by. She looked sleepy. She looked beautiful. And I guess it's just a matter of enough time passing for you to see it. You've had to just wait for all the pain to go away. You've had to get through that period where no one could really help you, and then one day you just see her sitting there, same lady who's been there all along, and all of a sudden you know you're looking at your future. You're looking at the rest of your life.

Hilary Richman

Look, can I just say, I hated that part of my life. That part of my life just sucked. I mean, the idea. No one knew what to do with me. My mother was an army brat like me, but I don't think she ever really wanted me to be in the military. God, I hope not. My father did. He wanted me to be in the Navy, and he'd give me little planes which I always broke and had to hide from him. But my mother, I don't know. After my father left for Manilla, she took me out of Hammond and enrolled me at Hoyt, which was precisely the same thing, only in California. I just think it had been so ingrained in her from her own childhood that this was the way you dealt with a child growing up, which was to give them military structure, that that's what she did with me.

But I hated that place. I deplored it. I wrote this poem when I first got there. I was eleven years old and I wrote this poem for some English assignment. It stemmed from a dream I'd had. It was just this very vivid dream about people singing and it being a very painful experience, something like they couldn't stop singing even though their ears were bleeding. So I wrote this poem which I thought was excellent for an eleven-year-old about the military, and I gave it to my teacher. And I don't even think he read it. He just smiled and took it away from me. I ended up being called into the Colonel's office, the headmaster—the members of the faculty had to be called by military titles, even though most of them weren't even officers. So I go into the Colonel's office, with these fucking World War II maps on the wall, and he stands there and reprimands me for writing this what he called obscene piece of literature. This man is just marching around this office in these boots and yelling at this poor little eleven-year-old kid for writing a fucking poem. I couldn't believe it. I was eleven years old and I was surrounded by these completely ignorant fascist idiots.

And I would write these long teary letters to my mom telling her how miserable I was and begging her to get me the hell out of there. I used to literally sit at this public phone in this hallway in this dingy dorm, with these lobotomies running around rat-tailing each other. I would literally sit there every night having to read this disgusting graffiti all over the booth, just waiting for her to call. It was pathetic. She would come see me occasionally. She would come up from San Diego because she was so lonely too, but she never really talked about taking me out. They are such awful places. They're awful awfully horrible places. They step on your mind and fuck with you and ruin people. I have terrible memories of them. I guess I'm obviously bitter.

Toddy Boone

Eton and I went to see Grandpa Edwin in Philadelphia when I was about eleven. Dad said if we played our cards right, it would be the only business trip either of us would ever have to make. We stayed about three weeks. They were getting ready to sell Sullivan South, so the upstairs had all been cleaned out. Eton and I had the whole floor to ourselves. We slept in sleeping bags in this room that used to sleep about six nannies. It was a fun trip. It was different. We were treated like little princes and we had this whole big house to run around. We'd play moonball over the house and at night we'd watch TV with Grandpa, and Eton would make up songs on the piano for him.

But the last night there, we were up in our room in the sleeping bags just talking, and Eton said he bet that Dad and Anne had been spending nights together while we were gone. I was pretty shocked. I said, "What are you talking about? They wouldn't do something like that." And Eton just said, okay, let's bet. He said it was probably the only reason we were there in the first place, just to give Dad and Anne a chance to spend the night, but I told him he didn't know what he was talking about. He was just being a jerk. So we bet. We hooked pinkies up there in our sleeping bags.

We didn't really resolve how we were going to figure out who was right, but Eton just said we'd know, and we did. The first night back we knew. Anne made dinner for us. She brought over a meatloaf, but when she came in Dad didn't even get up and go to the door. He just stayed in the living room, but it wasn't just that. It was the whole dinner, the way it felt. I remember looking at Eton during dessert. He was tonguing his spoon at me.

Joe Boone

I tried to talk to him about it. I tried to tell him that Anne and I were taking it easy. We weren't rushing into anything. I wanted to be honest with him. I wanted him to know, and he'd nod and say fine, but the whole thing still felt rotten. There were stretches there it seemed like he was never home, but we still felt like we had to sneak around. She'd have to tiptoe in, because we didn't know, he might have been up there. We didn't want to make a noise. If she was over visiting, we'd just sit in the living room sipping our drinks. Even when we went out to dinner, we'd find ourselves whispering. And he said to me once—I'd been trying to sit down and explain it to him—he said, "Don't tell me it isn't romantic, Dad." And I wanted to say, "Dammit, Eton, it isn't romantic. It's not romantic with you up there with your door closed, like we're just trying to hurt you. Anne cries." Jesus, she wanted to get to know him so much, I'd tell her what a great kid he was, but we're still having to sneak into the kitchen to touch each other. Two years of that, and that's what still stinks. Anne and I look back at these years, and we should be seeing how happy we were and how grateful we were for each other, and all we can remember is feeling like criminals in our own home.

Hilary Richman

Joe Boone was an asshole. He really was. I'm sorry. I hate for my mother's sake to say that I don't like him, but we all know I don't like him. He was just so full of shit. I couldn't deal with his father act, and Mom knew. But she would practically confide in me, just because I guess she had no one else. That was probably a mistake. You know, you've got your mother calling you on the phone saying, he's invited me ballroom dancing, and what was I going to say? Great, Mom, wear your taffeta blouse? I mean, the most I could say was, Mom, do what makes you happy. And what makes my mom happy actually, what she told me, is being allowed to tell someone, "Why don't you wear that shirt?" Well, Jesus, here I am, I'm a twelve-year-old fuck-up at the other end of the phone and my mom's telling me, you know, it's the little things, and I just go, Mom, if it makes you happy, go ahead. I just pretended I didn't care. It was fine. It's what she wanted. But I really objected to Joe Boone. Maybe I was too young to know it in so many words, and I certainly had no objections to Toddy or E.B., who I hardly even saw, but I never trusted Joe. Not that he ever trusted me.

God, I remember this Christmas vacation. I brought a friend home to San Diego. I guess I was the equivalent of a freshman, thirteen, and I had basically one friend. His name was Frisbee. He was a complete freak. All he did was play Frisbee and do drugs, and his mind was just completely gone. I thought he was fascinating. I don't know what the fuck he was doing at Hoyt in the first place, but he was just the best to hang out with. I think he was like an Eisenhower or something. Frisbee Eisenhower. But he'd been completely tripping at some school function so they put him on probation and his parents had basically told him to fuck off, so I said well, come to San Diego with me, and he did.

He came down with me for the Christmas holidays, and Christmas day we all drove to Joe Boone's house so we could pretend to have Christmas. It was something to just laugh at. E.B. was hardly even there. Joe Boone had gotten my mom this scarf, and Frisbee and I escaped out to the back lawn with this flask he took from Joe Boone's liquor cabinet. We got completely smashed, and I think Frisbee actually pissed on these flowers they had.

But Joe Boone came out and started yelling at this kid, who was obviously fucked up in the first place. Joe Boone was just incredibly mean to him. He was yelling and yelling and telling him that he'd ruined Christmas, he was intruding on a family Christmas, and he certainly made me feel that way too.

We went back inside finally, and my mom was there, and Joe put his arm around me. He gave me this transistor radio. What an asshole. I'm sorry, but he was.

II

Europe

Peter Finney

My father told me once, Beware the man from nowhere. Beware of him as a character in a play and beware of him in real life, because in either case, he's capable of anything. No family. No home. No mark on him. He's a knock on the door. You rush to it and through the peephole you see him, someone unfamiliar, twiddling his thumbs, whistling at the sky, innocent. Beware.

What a wonderful, horrible, humbling moment, to have spent your life as I had, having to resort to effects when I was at a loss, as I so often was, a scowl to effect my disdain for it all, and then to have a mere boy enter your life, stage right, and demonstrate an ability, such an ability. You could feel it in your throat each time he would do something new, My God, he's touched with two such precious things—instinct and independence.

So prepare to be humbled, my father should have told me. Let the stranger in, by all means, but pray that he's courteous, pray that he's younger and that he aspires to younger roles, because having to compete with him stroke for stroke—and this elaborate warning we conjure from my father, mind you, the great Franklynne—don't compete with him stroke for stroke, Peter, because this boy from nowhere, with no home and no legacy, has no limitations either. He can sound like anything, look like anything, act anything. So beware. Be wise. Take him under your wing.

Levi Mottl

We were in Europe together about six months. We made a sort of circuit, starting in Amsterdam and then swinging around the continent clockwise until we hit Paris in the winter. Joe and Anne announced their engagement sometime in the fall, when we were in Italy. I'd called Joe from a post office in Florence. He said he wanted to talk to Eton about it, but Eton wasn't with me. He'd taken the day in Siena, and I told Joe I couldn't promise Eton would return his call. They hadn't spoken the whole trip. Joe said fine, he didn't insist.

I told Eton that same night, in our pensione. We were lying in twin beds separated by a table lamp down on the floor, and I didn't really understand his response, except that after he was finished and we'd turned off the light, I suppose it was the first I realized he wouldn't be going home. He told me about Blue's Christmas presents.

Blue had died just before Christmas, and she'd had presents for them all. Eton said there'd been a painting for each of them and a present too. She'd had Claire do her shopping, and Christmas day they all opened their paintings together, just the family. Eton's was one of the ones she'd done in New Mexico, a gas station with a range of violet mountains behind, which Eton ended up putting over his desk. But after they'd all opened their paintings, which Eton said hadn't been a lot of fun, only he and Toddy had opened their presents, shirts that Claire had bought in Santa Barbara. Joe didn't open his. Eton said Joe just left it under the tree, and later he'd put it up in his closet. He never opened it, and Eton said he'd asked Claire once what was in the box, and she'd told him there were wine glasses, two of them, that Blue had asked her to get. Eton said every time he saw Joe drinking wine, he always thought about the two glasses Blue had bought for him, sitting up in his closet. He said he thought about the wine glasses they had downstairs in the cupboards breaking, and Joe would go out and buy more, and he'd never know that there were two up in his closet, waiting for him, from Mom.

Harry Hampton

Okay, I first met him at Harry's Bar, of course, in Paris. This is pretty near the end of the continental portion of his trip, when he's just hitting his stride as a traveler, by which I mean he's realizing people aren't sticking to him. I don't remember who I was with—whom—some nose job whose dad knew Art Buchwald probably, but I was in Harry's when they come in, tail end of the Frommer trip, Boone and Levi—hard to believe it was Levi because he didn't make much of an impression on me, but later, years later when we're in New York, Boone said it was. Anyway, they practically still have their backpacks on when I first see them, and Boone's young. He's younger than me. What the first note says is, "He acts like he's just grown into his skin and he's taking it for a spin, ninety miles an hour."

Okay, now I don't know how much that does for you. Probably not a lot, but what's more interesting than what the note says is that there's a note there in the first place. Back in Paris, see, I used to carry two notebooks with me. I was working at the *Herald-Tribune,* two years out of college, had a place on the Rive gauche, a pretty nifty setup, and I carried two notebooks with me wherever I went—one for reporting, which means checking quotes with Reuters, and one for fiction, which means shit. I was still writing fiction, and I used to take notes—images, ideas, comments, anything I thought I might be able to use in my writing. You know, "ideas are like birds," I'm saying to myself, "and if a pretty one flies by, you've got to have a pen around to shoot it down." That, needless to say, is a note, dated January of 1965, so I'm twenty, twenty-one years old.

But also and most important is, I'm taking notes on people. As far as I'm concerned, anyone I meet is fair game. If I have lunch with some Yugoslavian chef I'm interviewing for the paper, I take my reporter notes, but when we're finished, there's a good chance I streak home, pull out my fiction notebook and write down some really ballsy description of his nose. "His nose," say, "looked like a baked potato," ha-cha-chaa. So if you look in these notebooks, Hampton's Parisian period—and there's a good half dozen of them—that's what you're going to find for the most part, just little one-two punches on anyone I happened to meet. Say, "Pierre"—or no, "Girard," who was a real weasel, "Girard will push his mind only as far as it can easily go, but no further. Not where sweat's involved." You know, all as if someday I'll walk underneath a trolley car, some cop will find the notebook in my pocket, read it, rush it over to Methuen, and before you know it, they're giving guided tours of my mother's icebox.

Anyway, the point is, I took notes on Boone too—I couldn't help myself—but I'll tell you something, no one ever made me feel like a cheaper whore doing it. That first night in Harry's, Levi'd gone back to their hotel, and the two of us went out for a walk, out around the Latin Quarter, and even right there I'm feeling it. I've known the guy three hours, and I've already got this crotch-ache ambivalence going. Part of me wants to get back to my room right now and get something down, like "he's grown into his skin" or another one I'll share with you. Say, "B. sweeps in like a jet airplane, with all the noise and from the same height, content to watch his shadow flicker across the land," tra la.

Okay, but the question is, do I want to be doing that, or do I just want to walk down the goddamn street with the guy? This is my problem. This is my condition. I'm chronic, and basically I'm always trying to do both, within and without. "Does that not explain," I wonder, "the distant aspect of all the greats?"—a note. But am I great? Is this how it's done? Well, you tell me. You hear the notes. No. The notes are an embarrassment, and they do real violence to most of the people they're trying to describe. Because

Boone, for instance, was not, he never was, and I'm frightened to death there are people out there who are going to tell you he was, but he was not walking around in some cape like he's the second coming of Lord Byron. He did not have rocks in his pockets, and he did not howl at the moon. But the problem is, if you take a look at my notes, if someday there's a lucky trolley car and the notebooks do get published, you could end up thinking that, and I just want to get it said now that that's not Boone. That's a kid who wanted to write too damn much. That's me.

I mean, that first night, we went over to the Île de la Cité really late, and we were talking about Europeans or something. We're behind Notre Dame on one of the small streets. We see a party spilling out maybe twenty yards in front of us. People are leaving a party, and there's light on them, street light, and all of a sudden on our right, we both look up and there's a woman leaning out her window, second story. She was probably only four feet above us, but she had the window open, and the lights were off in her house. She was wearing a white slip and carrying a little dachshund in her arms, and she was crying. Beautiful, but she was crying, and then she pulled back inside. We didn't stop. We just kept walking, and I could hear her rattling the window. She was having trouble with the lock, but Boone was moving us along, past this thing, this vision. I didn't know what was up. Finally I had to say to him, "Could you hold on a minute?" And I stop and I take a note, which I happen to have here—"The dog's ears flapped like angel's wings"—and Boone just stood there waiting for me while I was writing, standing right there in the middle of all these people adjusting their collars. That's not a note. That's a memory.

Levi Mottl

The only time Eton and I ever really got the chance to paint together was in Europe, and I always thought that was too bad. Eton said something in his book about painting the same landscape with someone you care for—when you've finished painting together, there's a sort of silent pact that's formed between the two of you and whatever you've both been looking at, the buttress of a cathedral or a drift of blue lupin. It's not something that really hits with everyone, but it did with Blue, and it did with Eton.

The best work I have with me is from Bakken, which is an amusement park for the people of Copenhagen. It's very torn and tattered, much more picturesque than Tivoli, and if you get there the right time of year, the walk there is shaded by a canopy of intensely green trees, and that's where Eton and I stopped to draw the passersby. It must have been May or so, June.

Eton was always more interested in passersby, in human figures, than either Blue or I. Art was more of a speed sport for him. He never really had the patience for less fluid structures like architecture or even nature, and that really did set him apart from Blue. Blue was so concerned with the blocks of color that make up a vision. For Blue, it was all sensual—a still life, a landscape, a human face, they were all just things that light hit on. But you have to have tremendous natural skills to see that. A teacher of Blue's—Oscar Greenough—he once put it that you have to have the open mind of a chess master.

At Bakken, I'd sketched a group of children standing on line at a snack stand. Eton came over and when he saw what I'd done, he said I seemed to have a pretty firm idea in my head of what a group of children looked like. It was sort of brash, but true. He said all my figures looked like they'd been stamped from the same cookie cutter. So I offered him my charcoal. I asked him to draw the figures and see if there wasn't a sort of family resemblance there too. I gave him my tree stump and wandered off to get myself a Danish cruller, one of those garlic-and-butter–drenched crepes, which actually gave me pretty rancid breath all the way through Denmark. When I returned to Eton, he'd already done five or six sketches. He ended up filling the whole sheet, and I actually brought them with me today.

You know, I was looking through these and deciding which ones to bring, and I really am glad I kept them. I don't think I'd want to look at any of them more than once a year. They're just sketches, but there's always something a little more personal about sketches—less space between the paper and the hand. If all paintings were as personal as Eton's sketches—as these right here

I'm having such trouble finding—I don't think we'd hang them on our walls.

But here they are. These are the Bakken sketches. The children had all kept circulating, but you could still match them up with Eton's drawings—maybe one was standing on line now, tugging on her mother's skirt here, or this little gentleman hiding behind the poplar. Eton had just been sort of skeet-shooting. And I remember watching his pencil dash all over the paper and him making a sort of show of it, like the men who twist balloons into poodles and giraffes for children. They say your hand can have a kind of intelligence, a memory for what it likes to do, its favorite steps, but Eton's hand was more like a marionette. It never looked like it had any ideas of its own, and it never would have confused one child's forehead for another. It was what Blue called having an honest eye. You can even see, right below where I've dated it here. June, '66. "The honest eye—children at Bakken."

I wish we'd been able to do more drawing like that, but Eton's interest flagged. He started playing games. In Hamburg, I remember we'd pitched camp in one of the squares and were painting a cathedral there. Eton was settled out in front of a hotel, right by some tables with flamingo pink umbrellas. He was about fifty yards away from me, catercorner across the square. I was painting an old man sleeping with a long pipe in his teeth and a covey of sparrows at his feet.

I took a break at some point. I went over to get chocolate from Eton's box. One of Blue's teachers when she first came to the coast told her to always bring bars of chocolate with her on painting excursions for a quick shot of energy. It's a habit she passed along to Eton and me. We'd always have chocolate around, and at some point midway through a session we'd take a breather and share a Tobler, just sit with each other until we were ready again. So I went over for a chocolate break and took a look at what he'd been doing.

I've painted and sketched out in public with a good number of artists, all with their own particular customs and manners—a Ukrainian, Louie Beklov from the League, who used to beat people away from his canvases with his brushes and flick his paint thinner at you for just glancing over his shoulder. I don't think Louie would've taken too kindly to what Eton had done. He'd painted the same man I had, but he'd tried to do it from my angle.

He'd tried to paint my painting, and that's a pretty prickly move. It's not something I'd really advise, and I was a little surprised when I saw it. But I think it was just a trick on his part, a game, trying to see what I'd been seeing. It was a way of making the whole experience a little more mutual. He just looked up at me with an expression on his face, a sort of "Pretty neat, hunh?" That was the sense. And wherever we'd set up for the rest of the trip, whether it was in an old train station in Bremen, or a small cottage in the Black Forest, Eton would set up far away from me, and at some point he'd try and paint what he thought I had going. And I let him. I'm not certain I'd let someone do that now, and it's hard for me to believe I ever did, but I did. For one reason or another it didn't bother me. In fact, there was something kind about it, definitely kind I'd say, and something kind about my allowing it.

Harry Hampton

I'm trying to think of scenes. We drank a lot. We drank a *lot.* He was really a hell of a lot of fun to be with. I mean, I don't want to sound like Bacall on Bogie or anything like that, but I swear to you I've never met anyone with the ability he had to make you feel like, "Hey, where I was before, what I was doing before, that was shit, that was biding time. Here, sitting here with a little vino at the Luxembourg Gardens with the toy boats, this is where it's at." But what I wanted to know is, does he always have this much fun? I mean, the laughing. I can't stand it when people talk about laughing because it never works and you end up sounding like Jayne Meadows, but he, especially back then in Paris, Christ, did he make me laugh—the kind where you actually have to get down on the floor it hurts so much. I made him laugh too—I'm not saying I didn't have my moments—but he wasn't laughing as hard, and that was a little tough. I'm wondering in my notebooks, "Does he wish there was a tape recorder around the way I do?" Or, "How can he let these jokes go?" I even tried to write a few of them down. I did. Sure, there's something down here about forest animals, some routine he went into at the Tuileries about neurotic elk, and I can't remember it, but the truth is I don't care, because what I'd really like to have is the look on his face while all the milk is pouring out my nose. Seriously, he said something about Van Johnson's hair once at Nègre de Toulouse, I laughed some scotch through my nose and I haven't been the same since. But what I want to know is, was he laughing *at* me while this was happening? Was he laughing *with* me? What was he thinking? I don't know. I wish to hell I did, but I don't.

All I know is what comes through the notes, and what comes through if you read them all in one sitting, which I wouldn't wish on a Henway, is this recurring theme, and maybe it's just because I'm embarrassed at how hard he's making me laugh—I'm finding myself in a few too many defenseless positions—or maybe it's just because I was young, but "What in the hell is up with this guy?" I'm saying, "This is fun and all, but why does he put me on edge? What's the setup?" It was just a feeling, and I'm not going to be able to explain it—I can see that—but it got so bad I'd end up writing things like this, 12/8/66, "He never fails to give the impression that his mind is ready at any moment to wander somewhere that looks more interesting than me."

I think that's from Père-Lachaise. Absolutely pathetic afternoon. We'd been drinking somewhere, and we decided we wanted to go to the graveyard to look at all the famous people's tombstones. It's like a map of the stars' homes there—Chopin, Balzac, Oscar Wilde—Boone said he wanted to see it, so we went. It was probably late afternoon by the time we got there, and I'll level with you, the only reason I'd really gone was to show him these Hungarian bums that used to hang out by the tombstone of this heroic Magyar politician. Far and away the best material I'd found in Paris—I'd bought them a bottle of burgundy one time and they'd kissed my hands—but I wanted Boone to see them. So I'd edged us over, real casual-like. I acted like I hadn't even been thinking about it, but we stumble into these bums— surprise, surprise—and I tell Boone about the burgundy and what these people are doing there, what their story is, but Boone, I'm telling you, he looked so bored by the whole thing it was painful. All of a sudden his lids weigh five-hundred pounds, and I'll admit it, I was a little drunk and I took it personally.

So, after about a minute and a half of Boone standing there checking his watch, out of nowhere he says he's going to look for